IMAGINATION STATION

and other

STORIES AND POEMS

IMAGINATION STATION

and other

STORIES AND POEMS

selected by Pauline Francis

An anthology of winning stories from
the 2010-2011 World Book Day Short Stories competition

Published in 2011 by Evans Brothers Limited
2A Portman Mansions
Chiltern Street
London W1U 6NR

British Library Cataloguing in Publication Data
A catalogue record for this book is available from the British Library

ISBN: 978 02375 44447

Editor: Sophie Schrey
Designers:
Rebecca Fox, Evans
Jo Kennedy, Us2Design

FOREWORD

This is the first time I have selected stories and poems for the World Book Day/Evans Short Stories Competition. When the shortlist arrived, I was excited. I knew that you – the writers – would take me to places I could hardly imagine...

I was not disappointed. I've travelled to magical and mysterious worlds; to worlds past, present and to come; to worlds of horror and happiness. I've travelled by real trains and ghost trains. I've travelled under water and over water. I've flown, though not in an aeroplane. I've been trapped inside an egg – and bitten by fleas and vampires.

How did I select the stories and poems for this book? All those on the shortlist had good plots and original characters that made me want to read to the end. When I read them aloud, they had rhythm without too many adjectives and adverbs.

So – how? I waited... and waited. The stories that I liked best were the ones that I was still thinking about the next day... and the next... and I'm still thinking about them as I write this. For me, that's the secret of the best writing.

That's my advice: if you have time in your busy school life, wait to see if *your* writing grows.

Two special mentions? Theo Ross' *Solo* used

nursery rhymes to poignant and brilliant effect. And Joshua Jackson's *Rick in de Rapland* gave the reader this wonderful line: *"It ain't no shoes dat make YOU who you are."*

Thank you to all of you who entered the competition – and huge congratulations to the writers of this selection.

Keep writing.

Pauline Francis
Hertfordshire, 2010

ACKNOWLEDGEMENTS

Ten authors, two poets, twelve winners, 2500 schools and more than 3500 entries made this year's World Book Day Short Stories Competition the biggest and most successful yet!

We are delighted at the enthusiastic response to this competition, and impressed by the very imaginative entries, offering a rich variety of genres, from humour and dark tales to thought-provoking drama. We really appreciate the time and effort that go into each contribution, whether it is a story, poem or illustration, and hope that you enjoy reading these winning selections, primary and secondary, as much as we have enjoyed putting the books together.

The standard of writing was high, often outstanding – the judge's task was far from easy, but the final winners across the two age categories, ranging from 8 to 17 years old, deserve our heartfelt congratulations. Commiserations, too, to the runners-up – don't lose heart, remember that even the most successful authors weren't always published on their first attempt.

Many thanks to all the teachers and librarians who encouraged their students to take part and organised the entries; without your hard work this competition wouldn't exist.

A special thank you is due to the authors and poets who provided opening lines, and to their publishers. And to Pauline Francis who, for the first time, took on the difficult and unenviable role of Judge. Without Pauline, this competition would be an impossible task.

For all their hard work in helping to organise the competition, thanks go to Cathy Schofield of World Book Day, Truda Spruyt of Colman Getty and Jo Kennedy of US2 for the fantastic cover designs.

Keep an eye on www.worldbookday.com and www.evansbooks.co.uk for information about the next World Book Day Short Stories Competition.

Thank you
Evans Books

CONTENTS

‘Cath Solo became aware that something was missing early that morning, but it was already dark before she realised it was part of her own soul.’

Melvin Burgess

Duty

by Eleanor Cook

Cath Solo became aware that something was missing early that morning, but it was already dark before she realised it was part of her own soul. It felt terrible, as though a vital internal organ had been ripped out and replaced by a black vacuum. She felt empty, devoid of emotion. The sadness and disgust, the horror at what she had done would all come later, she supposed. But now she was just an empty shell, without part of her soul, lying on a bed in a small tent, right in the centre of nowhere land.

'Hey, Cath...', a fellow soldier poked his head through the tent flap, 'I just wanted to say... try not to worry too much. I know, it seems impossible, especially with it being your first time on a mission like that and all, but someone's got to do this job and it might as well be us.' He looked uncomfortable, not used to speaking about feelings and emotions, Cath supposed. She was grateful for him being there, though, showing some kindness, some sympathy. He, after all, must have gone through the same thing at some point in his career.

'When you first killed, how did that make you feel?' asked Cath, her voice just a few decibels above a whisper. A haunted expression flashed through the soldier's eyes, a painful memory had been stirred.

'Well, at first I didn't really feel anything. I... I was hollowed out, empty. Then, after a couple of days, I began to feel the pain and guilt, like a delayed reaction or something.'

'Do you ever get used to it?'

'To what?'

'To killing.'

The soldier sighed, his eyes on the floor, 'Kind of. After a bit you sort of realise that it's your job to be killing these people, and somebody else would do it even if you didn't, that they're going to die and it doesn't really matter who pulls the trigger.' Silence swept through the tent, neither had anything more to say. With a brief smile at Cath, the soldier ducked out of the tent.

Did everybody who killed lose part of their soul, wondered Cath. Was she surrounded by men and women who were missing a chunk of their spirit, or was it just her? The events of the night before kept replaying themselves in her mind, like a song on repeat, forcing her to live the awful moment again and again. Once more she had to endure the mental playback of getting into the helicopter with the rest of her squad and...

Cath Solo was crammed into the back of a helicopter, surrounded on all sides by sweaty bodies and powerful explosives. The target of the explosives was a building known to be a relatively important base for the enemy; one of the many attacks trying to break the stalemate between both sides. All the other soldiers whispered that it was just a desperate attempt to make some progress. The helicopter flew quickly through the darkness (the mission was undertaken at night, so as to avoid being seen), racing silently over the scrubland. Eventually, it landed approximately one kilometre from the target. Cath leapt out carrying a large amount of explosives and a heavy gun, which she prayed she would not have to use.

The soldiers ran through the night until they reached the outskirts of an ancient, crumbling town. Here, they crept through the streets, mere shadows in the dark, towards a squat, ugly building in the village centre, a harsh, concrete square quite unlike the surrounding houses. The soldiers split up into pairs and, silently, encroached upon the building from all directions. Cath came up from the south-east, tip-toeing after a fellow soldier. They positioned the explosive and primed it for detonation; so easy, Cath thought, to cause so much destruction. Their job complete, Cath and her companion sprinted from the building and took shelter behind a clump of small houses some distance away. They covered their ears and prepared for detonation.

'Thirty seconds 'til detonation!' The voice of Cath's squad leader crackled through her radio headpiece.

'Twenty-five seconds...'

The enemy base was surrounded on all sides by houses. Which people were sleeping in. How ma–

'Twenty seconds...'

How many people would be killed by this blast? How many of the casualties would be innocent people, just unfortunate enough to live near the base?

'Fifteen seconds...'

Would any children be killed?

'Ten seconds...'

Probably, almost definitely.

'Five...four...three...'

Cath's thoughts tumbled wildly through her mind. She was about to become a murderer.

'Two... One!'

The building erupted into a ball of flame. Cath felt the sheer energy of the explosion on her cheeks, sensed its raw power. Then the building began to burn. The ever-hungry fire devoured it from the inside out, leaving nothing but the crumbled concrete casing.

It was over. The soldiers raced from the town and into the helicopter, ecstatic from their success. The helicopter hummed in a wide arc, then began the flight back to base. It had ended.

Then Cath, lying in her bed back at camp, was forced to relive the worst part of the whole experience. As she turned to run to the helicopter, she glimpsed, through the smoke and flames, a young girl, only about five or six. She was crouched, crying, over the still body of a boy, slightly older.

That moment, Cath knew, was when she had lost part of her soul. She had caused the death of a child. It was unforgivable.

Eleanor Cook, aged 14
Oundle School, Northamptonshire

Solo

by Theo Ross

Cath Solo became aware that something was missing early that morning, but it was already dark before she realised it was part of her own soul. She must have been lying there all day. Her whole body ached. There was that hollow emptiness at the pit of her stomach that she had felt earlier. Her eyes were heavy beneath the bright lights. She was still groggy from the anaesthetic. She knew these were just the after effects of the operation. But the way she felt was not normal. Something had gone forever. Something was missing. She shuddered and put a shaking hand to her heart: 'My God,' she whispered, 'what have I done?'

Cath had never felt so alone. She closed her eyes tight, trying to shut out the light. She longed for a darkened room, but at that moment the curtains were ripped open and her bed was surrounded. There was the consultant, Mr Picket, his junior doctors in their stiff white coats hovered around him. And there was her husband, standing a little way off. He was holding Molly and had that anxious look on his face. Cath knew that look well. For months and months now he had carried it around. Through every appointment, every pill and injection. It was a look that haunted her in her sleep.

Meanwhile, their beaming daughter, Molly, was clutching her book of nursery rhymes. They had given it to her over a year before, when all this had started – something to keep her occupied during all the hospital visits. Its colourful pages had got them through many a consultation. Twelve months on, it was dog-eared and torn. Molly knew all the rhymes by heart. That book was her most prized possession.

'Rub-a-dub-dub, three men in a tub.

And how do you think they got there?' she sang as the doctors crowded round. *'The butcher, the baker, the candlestick-maker...'*

'Well, Mrs Solo,' chirped the consultant brightly, 'you'll be delighted to hear that everything went according to plan. The procedure went smoothly – a technical triumph, if I say so myself. Textbook stuff.' He smiled at her as he had done in all their consultations. A strangely thin, unconvincing sort of smile. He always seemed so pleased with himself, she thought. But perhaps that was to be expected. Doing what he did, day in, day out – a bit like playing god.

Deciding which should live and which should die. Bargaining with the soul.

'There was a crooked man, who walked a crooked mile,' sang Molly. *'He found a crooked sixpence upon a crooked stile.'*

With his shiny, white teeth, tailored suit and slick presentation, Mr Picket reminded Cath more of a game-show host than a doctor. Except that this was not a game. This was real life. And now, she realised with a sudden horror, it was all too late. She had made her decision. That part of her soul was gone. The emptiness welled up inside her and Cath felt that dull ache again. Mr Picket was addressing his students now, with his winning smile. He was giving them a potted version of her 'medical history'. Cath heard her long and painful struggle to have another child expertly summed up in a couple of short sentences.

'I had a little nut tree, nothing would it bear...' sang Molly in the background.

Cath closed her eyes and remembered her meeting with Mr Picket the week before. It was then that she had agreed – on an ordinary Tuesday afternoon. There was no rain, or thunder claps – just the usual dull, grey clouds hanging over the hospital. It was then that she had signed away part of herself. Lying on the bed in the consulting room, looking up at the black and white screen. She had stared at the tiny forms squirming in front of her. It was all so unreal. Like watching something on telly. The screen was just a fog. It was difficult to tell what was what. Mr Picket – ever helpful – identified different areas on the scan. With clinical precision, he pointed things out in the greyness. A stump of an arm. A leg. A tiny head. A miniscule heartbeat pumping in the dark. Smiling all the while, like a weatherman indicating the arrival of a high pressure and a particularly 'cold front'.

'Incey Wincey spider, Climbing up the spout.
Down came the rain and washed the spider out.'

'Observe, here, Mrs Solo,' Mr Picket had begun. 'There are three heartbeats. Not uncommon in these circumstances, believe me.

All in all it was a highly satisfactory result. Look on these 'extras' as an added bonus.'

'Baa, baa, black sheep, have you any wool?
Yes, sir, yes, sir...'

She stared at the screen, at the three tiny heartbeats. She looked at the 'extras' as he had put it, and in the family room next door, Cath could hear Molly's voice singing faintly in the background:

'There was an old woman who lived in a shoe.
Had so many children, she didn't know what to do.'

'However,' Mr Picket continued, 'in these situations it is advisable to consider the safety of the mother, and the optimum outcome for the child. Multiple births are rather complicated for a woman of your age. There is much more of a chance of a successful outcome if only one embryo is selected for full term.' He paused and smiled as if it was an advertising break, 'I'm sure you understand.'

Then came the full force of the question. Cath realised what she was being asked to do:
'Of course, the decision is yours. Should you wish to make the selection.' Again, Mr Picket leaned over her. Her heart skipped a beat and she gasped. "The selection" – he made it sound like a luxury box of chocolates. Her eyes opened wide as she took it all in.

'Eeny-meeny-miny-mo,' sang Molly, *'catch a tigger by its toe.*
If he squeals, let him go. Eeny-meeny-miny-mo.'

'I appreciate this is a difficult decision for parents to make. So you take your time to think about it.' The consultant made his way towards the door, 'I'll come back in five minutes.'

Cath turned to her husband. There was that anxious look again. She remembered how their eyes had met in the silence. He seemed completely lost.

'Goosey, goosey gander, where shall I wander?
Upstairs and downstairs, and in my lady's chamber...'

The tiny wriggling forms were there on the screen. Cath Solo closed her eyes and tried to get a grip. With a sick, sinking feeling she knew what she had to do. From next door came the unmistakable sounds of Molly's singing:

'Two little dickey birds, sitting on a wall, one named Peter, one named Paul.
Fly away, Peter! Fly away, Paul!
Come back, Peter! Come back, Paul!'

Theo Ross, aged 11
New College School, Oxford

‘I haven’t bitten you for days…’

Marcus Sedgwick

The Cellar

by Briony Davies

'I haven't bitten you for days...' When your brother hasn't spoken for two years you hope the first thing he says will mean something. After two years of round-the-clock care and daily therapy sessions, I'm not being unreasonable in wanting to hear something which makes sense, am I?

'Lena, you're the best sister ever!' would have been great, obviously, but I don't want to be too ambitious. Even, 'Where am I?' At least then I'd have been able to see some hope. But, 'I haven't bitten you for days'? Thanks, James, that makes no sense at all.

Mum was annoyed when I mentioned this, too. Apparently 'speech of any kind is an incredible breakthrough', but really, it's not. The only thing that statement taught us was what we already knew: James is a lunatic. Before he spoke, we could hope that deep down he wasn't crazy, that underneath the madness he knew who he was but just couldn't say it...

I shouldn't use words like 'lunatic 'or 'crazy';

the doctors say things like 'mentally deficient' or 'cognitively impaired', but I figure 'mad' sums James up better. He was never exactly politically correct himself, so I doubt he'd care about people calling him 'loopy', anyway. Once, he'd call anyone any name under the sun – when he was okay. When he was wickedly intelligent, with a warped sense of humour and a fierce, scary loyalty to Mum and me; the brother I idolised and adored in equal measure.

What gets me is that there never seemed to be any *reason* for things to change. You hear stories of people going nuts after a traumatic experience – rape, losing a loved one – but it was just a day, a normal day. A Monday, and I came home fuming, ready to regale James with tales of my draconian French teacher, and then. And then, and then, and then. I opened the door, and my life changed. James was curled up on the sofa, with no shirt on, sobbing and unable to understand a word I said. Hell, he didn't even seem to realise I was there. And he hasn't spoken since. Well, he hadn't, until yesterday. The doctors agree with my mum (thereby proving her wrong, because really, how much do doctors know? Their attempts to make James better certainly haven't worked) and reckon this change might signify a turning point in his recovery, so I'm supposed to spend more time with him, talk about childhood memories and things, try and trigger a reaction. It's not like I don't normally visit James – well, okay, I probably don't go as often as I should. It's just that some days I really can't face it, some days I can barely look at the broken man who sits staring into space, the man who looks so much like my brother but is a poor substitute.

Misgiving pushed to the back of my mind (or the middle, at least), I open the white doors and walk in. 'James? It's me, Lena,' I say, my voice sounding thin, scared. I get nothing. He just sits there, looking out of the window but I doubt he's seeing the view. I sit opposite him, talk about trivial things, *try*, but James never responds. He's as unreachable as if he were on the moon, but he's right here and it's so frustrating. Looking at him hurts, because he's James, but James gone wrong. James drawn by an artist who had never met the real deal. I drop my gaze – his face is hardest to see, vacant as it is – and notice the scars, visible on his arms and chest. The scars. Bite marks.

That day, James' arms and torso were covered in cuts – teeth-shaped cuts. We were baffled, the doctors were, too. In the end, the doctors stopped trying to work it out (like I said, doctors know nothing). But James said something about biting... maybe that sentence wasn't as random as I thought. Maybe it actually meant something. Something important.

'James. What are these?' I ask hesitantly. No response, naturally. I gently stroke a scar. Still he doesn't look at me, but he does yank his arm away. Progress? 'Who bit you?' I ask with a desperation that surprises me. In a way, I link the scars to his condition. If I can work out where they come from… things could change.

'I haven't bitten you for days.' It's terrifying, the way he says it. Monotone, no inflection, like a character in a horror movie. His eyes are huge, like holes in his gaunt, pale face, and the hair which was once so carefully styled hangs lank and matted. In essence, he looks like the madman he has become. *Why?*

I try to find out for an hour. He looks like he wants to tell me, is trying to reach through the veil of lunacy to make me understand, but can't quite get there. By the end of my visit, he's said one more word.

'Cellar.'

Now what on earth is that supposed to mean?

Obviously, the answer lies in a cellar. Maybe not – it could be a random word from the head of someone who doesn't know who he is, but it's all I have. The question is, whose cellar? Our house doesn't have one. There's one at school, I guess, but James was at home that day… our next door neighbours have a cellar, that'd be the closest one to where James was, but… hang on. There's a cellar next door. Our houses are identical. So where's our cellar? And just like that, I know. The bookcase.

The bookcase is a big old thing, nailed to the wall. James never liked it; I always loved it. I feel around the back of it – it's not nailed to the wall anymore. James. But why? Just out of curiosity I push it to the side, and there it is. Cellar door. A shiver runs down my spine – why would anyone hide a cellar? The bookcase was here when we moved in, what did the previous owners leave down here? And I feel the first breath of fear – because if what's down there sent James round the bend, I can't go down! But I have to, because if I don't I'll always wonder. The door opens easily, and I peer inside. It looks innocuous, so I tiptoe down. There's a piece of material on the floor – a t-shirt. Ripped down the centre. Bloody. James'. Before I can process that, I hear a voice unlike one I've heard before.

'I haven't bitten anyone for years.'

I turn to run – that voice isn't human. My brother came down here, and what happened sent him so far into his mind he can't get out. And as I slip on the stairs, as teeth close around my ankle, as I feel myself dragged downwards, as I scream even though I know no-one's there to hear me… I know I won't be as lucky.

Briony Davies, aged 17
Parmiter's School, Watford

Lilia

by Saffron Lowsley

'I haven't bitten you for days...' The small girl spoke absentmindedly to her fingers as she studied them. The minute slivers of nail had grown, now protruding from under the coat of red lacquer she had applied several days previously. Lilia wasn't into all that girly stuff. She'd only painted her nails to see what it looked like, but now had no remover to clean them. Despite the bottle claiming that it was the toughest varnish around, within hours, Lilia had managed to chip almost all of them. The ragged, bitten edges of nail were sharp, and dug into her palms when she clenched her fists. She clenched them now, against the biting cold of the wind.

From the top of the oil drum, Lilia liked to fancy that she could see the world. She would see rows and rows of never-ending houses, neat little squares set out on a game board. To her left would be Europe, and she would see the Eiffel Tower, Rome and its Colosseum, Mount Olympus, bullfights and matadors. And to her right, that was the Americas. Chocolate farms and, well, her knowledge didn't really stretch beyond that. In actual fact, all her eyes devoured was what they'd always seen: the scrap yard. Nothing more, nothing less.

The dump was dying. Slowly rotting into the ground. It was practically disintegrating at that moment. Iron claws snagged and bit at the earth as abandoned machinery lay to rust and waste away. Maybe in some hundred years they would be considered artefacts, relics of another lifetime. Washing machines sprawled on their sides, doors hanging open on weakening hinges. Some had deposited their entrails on the dusty earth, mismatched items of clothing, in varying degrees of decay, strewn all over the place, but never far from their host.

She stood atop the oil drum with an air of great importance. Looking down upon her kingdom, she noted the great number of objects surrounding her, memorising each one of her loyal subjects. For she was their queen in this tarnished paradise. The crusader, defender of her land. She was Lilia the Great, and she would be remembered always by anyone who dared read her name in the crisp pages of a history book, or by anyone who listened to the television or radio. All of the presenters would be talking about her. About how amazing she was for her age, how significant her actions had been. They would talk for centuries.

A light breeze lifted her hair, sending the tight, chocolate curls into a wild frenzy. They span about her level head as she stared down into oblivion. An odd strand would sometimes obscure a flinty eye before being snatched away by the wind. As the air calmed, the curls returned to their positions, standing sentinel against her torso. Lilia was small for her age. Her wiry build gave her the all appearance of a coiled spring, without comedy.

The sun was fast retreating into the dusk of the evening. Long shadows were cast, blackening the golden earth. Lilia clambered nimbly down from the oil drum, tripping often as she descended the pile on which she had stood. Every now and then, something of familiarity caught her eye. There was the crumpled bicycle that was often her horse as she galloped through the western plains of America. The upturned fridge that acted as her carriage on fine evenings out, when Lady Lilia honoured her subjects by gracing them with her presence. Out here in her own little slice of fantasy, she could do anything. Everything had a new name and meaning; Lilia decreed it so. Nothing was ever the same as its ordinary counterpart, ever.

The small child skipped through the mountains of rubbish, aware of the closing dark.

She would beat it home, she decided. Upping her pace, she danced along the path. The soles of her pumps left light indentations in the dirt. Lilia sped through the twisted metal gate and onto the pavement. Her feet slapped hard against the concrete as she vaulted the low wall into her front yard, hands scraping the uneven brickwork.

The Strang house wasn't spectacular. It was the end of a long row of terraced houses, snaking all the way up the hill and cresting there. Lilia lived at number 57.

As per usual, the front door had been left slightly ajar, probably by Lilia as she had snuck from the house in the early evening. The girl slipped quietly inside the narrow door. She kicked off her pumps in the hall, careful to place them in the darkest corner, so as to detract from the telltale dust covering the leather. She was like that. Sneaky, clever in her own way. Unique.

No greeting met her as the child scuttled through the dingy hallway, bare feet skimming over the boards.

Lilia entered the kitchen, only to find it empty. The table was bare. That was nothing new; there was often a lack of food in the Strang house. The girl wandered through to their dump of a living room, crashing down on the sagging sofa. She stared at the blank wall, at the place where their television set would have been. It had been taken away almost a month ago, when they could no longer afford the licence. Since then, boredom had passed and imagination had taken over. That was how she had discovered her kingdom.

She dozed off after a while. Her stomach growled impatiently and in the depths of her partially conscious mind, Lilia was fighting the tiger that had made the sound. Her sword flashed under the Indian sun as it blazed down on them, scorching her skin, leaving shiny red, raw patches in its wake. The tiger pounced. With reflexes faster than those of her opponent, Lilia rolled away, a cloud of dust rose behind her, putting up a temporary wall between her and the threat. Blinded, the tiger stopped, sniffing the air, trying to catch her scent.

There was an ominous creak as the front door swung open. If it hadn't have been for the rusted hinges, Lilia would never have heard it. She sat bolt upright, as if someone had just electrocuted her. There was no light in the room and she was scared to get up and turn them on; scared that it was only her imagination and that she'd look stupid; scared that it was all real and that there was an intruder in the house.

Instinctively, her hand rose to her mouth. Her teeth snagged on the nail, snapping it. It dangled from her finger, still half attached. She knew she'd regret it, and hell it hurt, but she continued. That kind of pleasurable pain was what she felt now, repeatedly self-inflicted to ease the desire, only to be back to square one. Lilia couldn't shake the weight of gnawing disappointment from her stomach. All her efforts wasted. But still it felt good. She realised what a comfort it was, as her teeth tugged off the remaining sliver of nail. And right now she needed comfort more than self-restraint.

Saffron Lowsley, aged 13
Culcheth High School, Warrington

‘Thomas and Beth were having a perfectly normal ride home, until their train stopped at a station that didn’t exist.’

Rick Riordan

The Un-decided

by Ellie Sowden

Thomas and Beth were having a perfectly normal ride home, until their train stopped at a station that didn't exist. Passengers complained, the lights dimmed and that's when it started. Everything turned deadly quiet and then it was coming from everywhere, so loud it drowned everything else out.

Not knowing what else to do the kids clung to each other for comfort. What the hell was going on? What was it? Why wasn't it stopping? It seemed to be getting closer, and closer, closer towards them, but how was that possible? All the windows and doors were locked, nothing could get inside. Could it? The kids started to scream.

STOP.

The voice spoke, but only to Beth. She shivered.

STOP SCREAMING, IT'LL JUST GET ANNOYED.

Beth, still cradling Thomas, looked around. Where had the voice in her head come from? Thomas hadn't heard it. She shoved her hand over Thomas' mouth to shut him up and as she did the noise grew faint, until it was hardly there at all.

GOOD GIRL.

Where was this voice coming from? Whose was it? And what was going to get annoyed? Beth cradled Thomas tighter; he was shaking. She pulled him onto her lap, rocked him back and forth, trying to soothe him. Why did this voice make Beth go all tingly inside? She knew she'd never heard the voice before yet it seemed so familiar. It radiated all the way through her making her trust it and feel safe.

DON'T BE SCARED, I WANT TO HELP YOU. MY NAME IS ADAM. TAKE THOMAS TO THE BACK OF THE TRAIN, HE'LL BE SAFE THERE.

Beth didn't know what to do. Was the voice in her head telling her the truth, did it really just want to help her and Thomas, or was it lying? The voice seemed to know what was going on, it knew that screaming would annoy it, how did it know that? Did it also know what this thing was? It seemed to be more clued in than Beth right now. There was really only one way to find out what was going on. Beth picked Thomas up and started towards the back of the train. Where was everyone? All the other passengers had disappeared; no one else was on the train. Beth and Thomas were alone. Beth lay Thomas on the back seats of the train and told him to go to sleep, that when he woke up they would be back at home.

WANT TO KNOW WHAT'S GOING ON? GO BACK TO YOUR SEAT. UNDERNEATH IT THERE SHOULD BE AN ENVELOPE. DON'T READ IT. BRING IT TO THE FRONT OF THE TRAIN, IT'S A KEY; USE IT TO UNLOCK THE DOOR.

Unlock the door? But wouldn't that mean that whatever was outside would be able to get in? Beth was scared, her skin was sweating, her head was dizzy and her feet felt heavy.

HURRY, THERE'S NOT MUCH TIME.

Beth could hear the urgency in the voice; it must be telling the truth, it couldn't fake that kind of panic. Something was about to happen, Beth could feel it in her bones, something wasn't right. Beth looked under her seat and picked up the letter, it was white with a black seal on it and the letter U printed in red. Without really knowing why Beth reached over the table and pulled up the shutter covering the window. What she saw astounded her, she couldn't believe it. White. The whole place was white. The trees, the grass, the sun, the sky, all of it was white. It looked like the inside of a mad hospital. Where was she?

THERE'S NO TIME FOR THIS. HURRY, BEFORE IT'S TOO LATE.

With one more quick glance outside Beth

hurried to the front of the train and then stopped. What would happen when she opened this door? Would she get sucked into this world of white, never to be seen or heard from again? Would whatever was out there grab her for reasons unknown? Beth had no idea what was going on, she was acting on the words of a voice she felt strangely connected to.

'Why?' Beth thought, feeling dizzy, wondering whether the voice could hear her.

WHY? JUST PLEASE, TRUST ME.

'Just tell me what's going on. I'm not going to open this door until I know what's behind it and where I am.'

YOU NEED TO OPEN THE DOOR, OTHERWISE YOU WILL BE TRAPPED HERE FOREVER AND IT'LL EVENTUALLY FIND ITS WAY INSIDE.

'Well a few more minutes isn't going to hurt anyone, please explain.'

Beth stumbled back to a chair. Feeling exhausted she slumped down into it. Trapped here forever? What about Thomas, she couldn't let that happen to him. She trusted this voice even though she had no logical reason to; she knew it would never lead her, or Thomas, to any harm.

'Who are you?' Beth asked the voice in her head.

MY NAME'S ADAM.

'Well Adam, how do you know so much about this place? And how can you speak inside

my head?'
I WAS IN YOUR POSITION LAST YEAR AND I GOT STUCK. ANYTHING'S POSSIBLE HERE, INCLUDING MIND READING, IT JUST TAKES A LITTLE PRACTICE.

'Where are we?'
WE'RE IN THE UN-DECIDED. I KNOW IT SOUNDS WEIRD, BUT EVERYONE COMES TO THE UN-DECIDED AT SOME POINT AND THEN SOME PEOPLE, LIKE ME, GET STUCK.

Beth didn't want to hear this, she wanted Adam to tell her this was a mad dream and if she wanted to get out all she had to do was pinch herself and wake up. Beth closed her eyes, leaned back on the seat and pinched herself as hard as she could. When she opened her eyes, she leaned over and looked out the window. Everything was still disgustingly white.

Wondering if Adam was still listening she thought, 'Fine, I'll do it.'
GOOD GIRL, GO GET THOMAS. DON'T TELL HIM ANYTHING; JUST SAY YOU'RE GETTING HIM OUT OF HERE.

Beth rose to her feet, feeling strangely refreshed. She jogged down to the other end of the train, picked up her little brother and carried his sleeping body back down to the door.

'One last question?' she asked Adam.
SHOOT.

'What's outside? What was making all that noise before? What didn't you want to make angry?'
THE LIGHT.

Adam's voice broke when he said the words. Beth didn't quite understand but she didn't want to push it any further. She just wanted to get her and Thomas out of there safely. Then it struck her: was Adam allowed to leave? Could he come with them?

WHEN YOU OPEN THE DOOR, YOU WILL HAVE TO JUMP STRAIGHT INTO THE DARKNESS BEFORE THE LIGHT HAS THE CHANCE TO GRAB YOU.
GO NOW!

Beth put the card in the door and watched it slid open. It was so bright, then suddenly a big circle of darkness slid towards her.

JUMP, NOW BEFORE IT'S TOO LATE.

Trusting a voice she didn't know, Beth jumped. The black engulfed her and Thomas. Beth closed her eyes. She didn't know where the darkness would take her and Thomas, but she trusted Adam. That was enough.

Ellie Sowden, aged 15
Barnard Castle School, County Durham

Imagination Station

by Katie O'Reilly

Thomas and Beth were having a perfectly normal ride home, until their train stopped at a station that didn't exist.

We were on our way home from our trip to the seaside just like we did every year. It was always how I spent my summer holidays. When we were younger we called them adventures. It was just Thomas and I, me and my best friend. The train ride home was always my favourite part of our trips. We could talk about anything and everything together so effortlessly. I could be myself around Thomas. We sat side-by-side on the train. Thomas let me sit by the window because he knew how much I liked to look out as we passed the water. We laughed and joked and played lots of games of snap as usual. Every train ride home was the same time and time again except one year when our train brought us to an unexpected stop.

I hadn't noticed we were the only people in the carriage until the train suddenly stopped. I knew every stop, every turn and every bridge the train went under as we took the same route to the seaside every year. This stop was new. I had never heard of this stop or seen it before. Curiously I checked the map above the train door. This station was nowhere to be seen. It was like it didn't exist. Just as I was going to sit back down the intercom came on. 'Final stop, Imagination Station, final stop'. This couldn't be right I thought. Our stop was two stops away; this couldn't be the last stop. The train doors slid open and Thomas jumped out onto the platform straight away. I didn't think it was such a good idea to get off at a strange station.

'Come on Beth, let's look around. We can wait for a train home. It can be our own little adventure,' Thomas said in a convincing way. He put out his hand and without any hesitation I jumped out after him.

The station didn't look like any other station. The platform had a pink floor and blue walls. The lampposts looked like the curly straws I had when I was four and the benches were made from what looked like a hundred colourful cushions. The main building at the train station had at least ten little windows and a huge door. The door was at least twelve feet tall and it had a doorknob the size of a beach ball. To me this didn't look like a real station. It looked more like something out of a cartoon.

'Maybe we should go home Thomas,' I suggested.

'The only way we're getting home is if another train comes; we'll just have to wait,' Thomas replied. Just then a small dwarf-like man came from the big door. I couldn't help but wonder how he reached the doorknob.

'Hey, could you tell us when the next train to Blanchardstown is?' I asked the small strange man.

'Oh hello, train home? Sorry, but no one leaves without taking a trip into their own imagination. Follow me children,' the small man replied.

He started to walk back towards the big door. Just as he reached the door he turned back and looked over his shoulder and said, 'My name is Michael.' As Michael walked through the big open door leaving it open, I turned to look at Thomas. He shrugged his shoulders and with ease followed the strange man.

'Come on Beth, adventure remember?' With that we entered the station together.

Although the outside of the station was bright and colourful the inside of the station was not what I expected. It was a black room with no windows. I wondered where the ten windows had gone. This place must be more magical than it seemed at first.

'So what do we have to do to go home Michael?' Thomas asked the small man who was now holding a candle to give the room some light. It was still just a black empty room. Michael began to explain where we were.

'This is Imagination Station. Everyone's imagination is different. Imaginations are like worlds inside our minds of all things magical and fun in our lives. People are sent to Imagination Station when they begin to lose all things childish and fun. Since you two are such good friends losing this childhood connection could ruin your childhood bond.'

'But we're best friends Michael, can we not just go home, this is pointless,' I replied.

'Young foolish girl this is now; time changes everything. You will soon be too old for your little adventures and going to the seaside will seem like a waste of time. I know it may seem impossible, but friendships sometimes end when your childhood ends.'

What Michael said began to make sense. I never saw Thomas at school anymore as we hung around with different groups. The only thing we did together was our trip to the seaside every year, our only tradition that lasted. We no longer went to the cinema or went on our bikes to that old scary house down the road. Was this our last chance to stay best friends? Thomas seemed to agree as he answered Michael.

'You're right, isn't he Beth? We don't spend as much time together as we used to. Tell us what we have to do and we will do it.'

Michael brought us to a door.

'This is the entrance to your imagination,' Michael explained. 'If you walk in holding hands you will see your combined imagination. This means it will show all the childhood adventures that made your relationship so close. Hopefully seeing your imagination will bring you closer and your childhood bond will be as strong as it was when you were younger.'

I asked Thomas if he thought we should go in to this strange room. 'Beth, if it means we become better friends like we used to be, definitely.'

I held out my hand, waiting for his. A second later his hand was in mine and we entered the room.

It was very dark at first. I was waiting for something to happen but nothing did. 'Is this it?' Thomas asked impatiently.

I couldn't see Michael but I heard him say, 'Wait for it... wait for it.'

It was then that I saw it. The burst of colour and fun. We were now in what looked like a pink cloud. It was fluffy, and it felt like a bouncy castle when we walked on it. All the things I loved from my childhood were floating around. Each one had a different story or memory attached to them. Like giant glasses of 7Up that we used to drink on the way home from the seaside, tennis balls for a game called T&B that we had made up when we were seven because we were bored. There were the hundreds of seashells that we collected over the years. So many memories came back to me. I had forgotten most of them. They were the happiest times of my life. I couldn't understand how I had forgotten such important things. One thing I noticed was that there were two of everything: two bikes, two tennis balls and two giant glasses of 7Up. All of these precise memories were shared with Thomas. I couldn't let our relationship drift apart anymore. The only way I could see our relationship staying as close as it was, was by our being a little bit more childish and bringing our childhood traditions back to life.

'Beth?' Thomas called.

'Yeah,' I replied.

'You up for a little adventure to the old house down the road? There are two bikes in my shed,' Thomas said, smiling.

'Sure. And there are two bottles of 7Up in my fridge,' I answered.

'Perfect.'

With that the room became dark again and

it started to spin. Recovering from my dizziness I realised where we were. I was by the window beside my best friend looking out the window at the beautiful water. We were on our way home to start our memorable traditions once again thanks to Michael and the Imagination Station.

Katie O'Reilly, aged 14
Hartstown Community School, Dublin

‘When viewed from one angle, the egg seemed very solid and opaque, but when Jarvis shifted around to the side he caught fuzzy glimpses of something moving behind the curved surface, something alien.’

Eoin Colfer

Life

by Emma French

When viewed from one angle, the egg seemed very solid and opaque, but when Jarvis shifted around to the side he caught fuzzy glimpses of something moving behind the curved surface, something alien. Seeing the shadow and its fleeting transition across the opalescent surface, his heart contracted with a mixture of fear and excitement that left it feeling heavy and his stomach slightly sick. You never saw eggs anymore; all animals were bred using in-vitro fertilisation in the laboratories of the Livestock District, to ensure the most efficient genetic material. He'd never seen a newborn animal either, only pictures on the holoscreen of his biology classes, but he remembered the lessons almost word for word and managed to hack into the Rationing System and gotten himself another two dairy coupons, so when it did hatch he'd be able to feed it. He'd reprogrammed his climate control too, so that the heating stayed on an hour longer than the District Authority allowed, in the hope that that combined with the blankets and shredded paper he'd wrapped it in would provide the needed incubation.

There was little more he could do, except take the pearly, polished sphere out of its bondage each night and watch for that movement, the signal that whatever was inside *was* still living, no matter how far the odds were against it. It had been nine days since Jarvis had found the bundle sitting in his work locker, and every day he expected the egg to be gone from its hiding place under his bed, or to have lost its moonlight shimmer, or for the shadow not to come. He was always surprised, yet always aware of his mounting crimes and the danger having the egg in his possession put him in – for no one outside of the Livestock District was supposed to know what life looked like anymore.

It was never said aloud, of course, but Jarvis knew, looking with silent reverence at the life in front of him, why this was the case. It was because things such as the egg, so full of the sheer wonder and mystery of existence, provided hope. They provided a purpose, and a sense of compassion that the Authority had long since wanted buried. The need to protect, to provide; all fought the neat and precise order the Systems presented to the Districts, the harsh, simple boredom of routine that chafed a person from their birth – through artificial means, of course – to their deaths, which ended with a plain black box, a plain black van and an unknown destination.

Jarvis looked at the beautiful, alive fragment of chaos in front of him, and was glad that whoever had decided he was to look after the egg had made the decision.

He wondered if the egg's sender had known about the application for District Migration he had made eleven months ago, to Livestock. Ever since Jarvis had taken his first biology class at the Secondary Education System, he'd been fascinated by the anatomy of living creatures, of the precise mechanics of their vertebrae, and their complex instincts, behaviours and sense of loyalty. Ever since he'd heard the term, he'd known he'd wanted to be a veterinarian, to look at the craft of each animal's body and then mimic and repair its precise sculpture, either in a breeding lab or growth facilitator. Did the unknown sender know of his illicit, black market purchases of large, outdated tomes of anatomical diagrams – filled with animals that had long been classed as unnecessary and were now extinct – as detailed as the blueprints he was forced to stare at each day, due to being assigned to the Technological District at birth, or of his Rationing System tweaks so that he received protein substitutes instead of meat, due to his new-found vegetarianism? Surely his obsession had something to do with his selection, though Jarvis kept all these thoughts of life and preserving it secret, so it unnerved him that anyone else could be aware of it.

Another glimpse of the shadow snapped him from his reverie, and Jarvis placed his hand against the smooth, supple surface, feeling the throbbing heat emanating from it. He wondered if it was the animal's heartbeat he felt between his fingers, or simply his own pulse magnified by the slightly pliant membrane stretched taut like the skin of a drum. He'd reread the books, but they mostly focused on skeletons and so they'd given no indication of which species of animal the egg would turn into. He also knew that, with the genetic engineering that was seemingly the law which the Districts lived by – using it to improve the breeding of crops, animals and humans – the egg's inhabitant was likely to be a species that Old World scholars knew nothing about. He'd heard such *stories*, muttered low amongst only close numbers, of experiments that had malfunctioned and had to be terminated, or of species that had become too successful and wiped out whole other test groups, perhaps even some of the scientists themselves. And then he'd heard the rumours, the ones that were somehow heard yet never spoken, about what projects the Authorities were performing; whole horror stories of crossbreeding and inbreeding and gene mutilation and synthesised natural selection, where the scientists decided which mutation would be more helpful to the Districts and terminated those without it.

The surface shuddered, a vague tremble that Jarvis wouldn't have noticed had his fingers not been pressed to it. His heart leapt. That was the second time in ten minutes; he'd had a feeling it was almost time, doing frantic calculations in his head, combining the time he'd possessed the egg and the estimated travelling time, from Livestock to Technology, maybe. He'd known the incubation period shouldn't last too long, for why should the scientists have to be left on tenterhooks by *nature*? There would be no waiting for the laboratories, for unlike an Old World painter who was willing to spend years on a masterpiece, they did not possess much patience.

Another tremor, this time within minutes of the first, and visible to the eye. Jarvis removed his hand and fought the longing to crack the egg open himself, instead telling himself to let things take their course. He'd barely had time to do so when another shudder moved the egg and the shadow became darker, more formed, as it pressed against its prison. The egg shuddered again, there was a splintering crack, it fell on its side, and, before Jarvis could reach out and stop it, rolled off the end of his cabin bed, to shatter on the floor. To reveal a baby.

Jarvis blinked, hardly able to believe it. He fought against a painful surge of bile. It was not an ordinary baby, not a human child, like the holoscreen pictures. Its skin was leathery, a deep bottle green, it had cold, golden eyes with slit, vertical pupils and a calculated intelligence. Most impossible of all, it had a long, reptilian tail, which coiled protectively around its torso at the touch of cool air.

The lizard child squinted at Jarvis and smiled, showing a metallic glint of sharp, pointed teeth.

Emma French, aged 16
Fulford School, York

Rebellion Avenged

By Jade Corbett

When viewed from one angle, the egg seemed very solid and opaque, but when Jarvis shifted around to the side he caught fuzzy glimpses of something moving behind the curved surface, something alien.

Suddenly, a loud noise echoed through his prison, throbbing through his head, making him gasp in pain. Jarvis hadn't heard anything but his own thoughts, which stopped making sense after the first decade, for over twenty years. The shapes were moving now, and Jarvis remembered something. He remembered that his sentence was not a life sentence, and that maybe, just maybe, he was finally free to go.

Memories flooded back to him, memories that he had struggled to recall, even after a superhuman effort. He had a wife called Sophia, and two children, Millie and Sam. But, just as quickly as it had come, the happiness trickled away, leaving only regret. Regret that he could not even remember their faces. Jarvis could feel the ice melting around him, and, for the second time, he shifted slightly.

A loud crash woke Jarvis, and he jerked in shock. He could move his arms. Before he had time to recover, the smooth surface of the egg splintered and caved in, covering him with shards of shell. Beams of light streamed in through the gaps, blinding him. When he could see again, Jarvis found himself staring up at a cloudy grey sky, surrounded by debris. Where was the high security enclosure, guarded by specially trained men? What had happened to all the other eggs, those containing every criminal in Britain?

Jarvis hadn't noticed it before now, but a number of creatures were crouching beneath what looked like trees, cocking their heads and hissing slightly. Staring, Jarvis could see features of his own race reflected in their faces. He shook his head, reminding himself that he didn't have talons or leathery black skin. As they turned their bulbous red eyes towards him, two of the creatures stood up. Jarvis' blood turned cold as they inched towards him, and then stopped about a metre away. 'Stand up,' one hissed, 'and look Millie in the eye.' Jarvis froze at the sound of his daughter's name, and rose to face them. His knees felt wobbly, but he was determined not to show any weakness to the beings. As he stared at 'Millie', he heard a gasp escape from her lips.

'That's him!' she whispered. 'That's my dad.'

Jarvis woke up. He was groggy, and the last thing he could recall before everything went black was the weeping face of his... daughter.

'Ahh...finally, you've come round! That's good. Now let me introduce myself. I am Patrick Riley. You may have heard of me.' Patrick crouched down to his level.

It was only then that the blurred edges of Jarvis' vision sharpened, and he could see that he was chained to a wall in what looked like a dark cave.

'You are the Member of Parliament representing my town,' he croaked.

'I was, but not now,' Patrick spat back. 'This is what's left of York, of England, of the world! And you're to blame!'

Patrick was shouting now. He took one last look of disgust at Jarvis, turned, and then stormed out of the room. Jarvis was drifting in and out of sleep when the heavy wooden door creaked open, and Millie was led in.

'I just wanted to see you, Dad,' she said, her voice barely a whisper. 'I wanted to tell you about... Mum, and Sam too. I thought you would want to know what happened after they caught you.'

'Yes.' Jarvis' eyes welled up with tears

when he thought of his beautiful wife, with her sparkling eyes, and his son, who was only a child when he last saw him. 'Tell me what happened. How did we end up like this?'

'You see, when you were locked away, people started copying what you'd done, thinking it brave. As you can imagine, the government had had enough. They executed anyone who was remotely connected to anything involved with the rebellion. They hunted us down. They murdered Mum before my eyes, and then Sam too. Then they gave me a choice. I could join the government or die. It was as simple as that.' Millie gulped, and then carried on, 'France joined the rebellion, and then Germany, and soon the whole world was in chaos. We evolved quickly, performing tests on ourselves that would keep us alive. The only reason your egg survived was because we stole it from the prison. It wasn't hard. All the guards had been killed and the security hijacked years beforehand. It was lucky we stole you when we did though, because the prison was bombed the next day. For years we've been trying to crack open that egg, but only recently have we found the technology to break through the layers of ice, nano titanium, and calcium composites. We kept you alive, Dad, just so we could kill you ourselves. You are the one who destroyed life as we knew it.'

'Do you want me dead, Millie?' Jarvis

grabbed her wrist, 'Would you let me suffer like that?'

Millie paused. 'Yes.'

Abruptly, she stood up and walked out of the room.

Patrick returned for him the next morning.

'What do you want?' Jarvis sighed, resigned to the fact that Patrick would always hate him, no matter how polite or rude he was.

'I just thought you'd like to know when your execution is,' Patrick smirked. 'After a lengthy discussion with our leader, we came to a decision.'

'Yes?'

'It will be on the twentieth of September.' Patrick gave another smug smile.

'So how many days have I got left to live?'

'Let's just say that you should savour today, because it's your last day on earth.'

A hard kick in the ribs woke him the next morning. Jarvis sat up groggily, and then paled as he remembered what day it was. Before his eyes had time to adjust, he was hauled to his feet and marched down a thin passageway, out into the open air.

An evolved human stood there waiting for him, holding an axe, and around him stood a crowd. Scanning the thronging mob of hybrids, Jarvis caught sight of Millie, her leathery skin looking tighter, and her eyes moist.

'I am addressing all of you gathered here today, to witness the death of the man who ruined our lives and caused the murders of all our loved ones...' the Executioner boomed, talking about how many sins Jarvis had committed, and how he should die without delay. Jarvis hung his head. Didn't they realise his loved ones were dead too?

After what seemed like a lifetime, Jarvis was dragged into the circle. Hard hands pushed down on his back, forcing him to the ground. His heart heavy, Jarvis looked up, and locked eyes with his daughter.

With a swish, the blade fell.

Jade Corbett, aged 12
Sidcot School, North Somerset

‘The noise woke everybody up – the sort of noise that sends you diving under the duvet.’

Pauline Francis

The Sound of Silence

by Rachel Davis

The noise woke everybody up – the sort of noise that sends you diving under the duvet. That's how it affected me anyway, I simply wanted to dive under the covers and cry my eyes out where no one could hear me. No one was asleep; they were all too busy listening. But it was silent. Silence meant no waves and no waves meant death, just as it almost had done on our first day…

The engines had been turned off as we reached our docking spot. The silence, that's what hit you. You've never heard a silence that complete. No wildlife, no wind, no waves, nothing. It was the first glimpse we caught of the hell beyond the thin layer of beauty. We fell into its trap. We couldn't break this silence, we simply couldn't. We stood frozen for many minutes getting dangerously cold, until a rope slipped out of the hands of a paralysed seaman, sliding into the icy water. That sound broke the spell. I think we owe our lives to that man; I never thanked him, never will now. For once the Captain didn't issue a reprimand about the loss of the rope. I think he alone understood what might have happened if that rope hadn't fallen. None of us wanted the silence to return so we set about creating our own little bubble of noise. Yet the silence remained, hovering just outside.

Discovery's bell clanged twice signalling the start of my watch. With a rap on my door the Captain stuck his head round. 'No change as yet Mr Wilson,' he told me, the fact that he used my surname the only indication of his internal strain.

'Aye, aye sir,' I replied before donning my outdoor gear and leaving the cabin.

On deck one could see the distant lights of the *Morning*; at one time she would have been a saving grace, now she seemed a herald of death. Looking over the side the ice came right up to the hull of the ship, trapping us so we couldn't move. Dispelling these gloomy thoughts from my head I clapped my hands together and began to pace in an effort to keep warm.

My watch continued without incident for about an hour. Now, I already knew my ears were sharper than the other men's; when searching for penguins I could always hear them before my helpers. I had paused for a moment at the prow of the ship looking towards where the sea was. My eyes followed the meandering rift in the ice made by manpower and explosives and then the barrier of ice we had yet to break through. We had been instructed to give up trying to free the boat and to trust the power of the sea. If waves were to come and break up the ice we could all go home; if no waves were forthcoming then *Discovery* would have to stay behind. It was then I heard it, a sound so faint it might have been my imagination. I couldn't tell what it was but I wouldn't let myself speculate for fear I allow myself a false hope leading to greater disappointment. I was confident the other men hadn't heard it, and a glance round the deck confirmed this so I resumed my pacing.

Half an hour later I had been joined at the prow by another of the crew when the sound came again. It was still faint but louder, loud enough for the seaman next to me to hear it. His eyes lit up with hope so I put an arm round his shoulder and turned him to face away from the crew. 'Don't tell anyone what you just heard,' I hissed. 'I don't know what it is and until we know you mention it to no one. If we were to tell anyone the crew would all come rushing up here to celebrate and if we were wrong can you imagine how angry they'd be about us getting their hopes up and just dashing them? Now look sad you or you'll make them suspicious. If you let on and we're wrong you might as well be dead, so keep quiet, do you hear me?' The poor chap nodded mutely, sufficiently quelled by the force in my voice. I didn't want to scare him but I had to impress on him the seriousness of the situation. I sighed and continued my patrol.

It came again even louder ten minutes later. So much louder that nearly all those on deck heard it and I had to convince them it was a hallucination. Those noises *were* beginning to sound more like ______; I wouldn't even let myself *think* the word. But, deep down, I *was* beginning to hope that these sounds might be what I wanted them to be. So unsure was I that I strolled, trying to appear nonchalant, down to the Captain's cabin to inform him. He listened intently to my words. 'We can't let the crew suspect anything. If we're wrong we'll have a mutiny on our hands you know.' I nodded. 'I would normally send a party along to investigate but we can't alert the crew.' He paused for a while to think before shrugging on his overcoat and strolling up on deck to have a listen himself. Neither of us wanted the crew to see that I had woken the Captain, even if they didn't know why. It gave them hope, hope that might well be unfounded. The Captain spent the rest of my watch on deck but the sound didn't come again. Not a word was spoken as we stood at the prow but even *I* heard nothing. The Captain knew I wouldn't lie about what I heard, the matter was far too important for that. However he couldn't rule out an overactive imagination and a pair of ears hearing what they wanted to hear. It was with a sigh and a regretful look in the direction of the sea that he gave the order.

'Pack your bags men and say your goodbyes, only a miracle could save her now.'

We knew the Captain wasn't a heartless man, he loved this ship as we did, and he wouldn't agree to leave her behind unless he felt that he had no choice and this was the right thing to do. I tried to turn the expression on my face into one of calm acceptance but I failed. It seemed that despite all my precautions about not allowing myself any hope, I still hadn't accepted that we might have to leave *Discovery* behind.

Packs of all shapes and sizes were being loaded on to the sledges to drag across to the *Morning*. Men were saying their goodbyes to this remarkable wasteland that had sustained them for these past four years. Deep down though I couldn't believe we were going to leave our ship behind. I waited until the last possible moment to pack my bags and did so with a heavy heart. We were on board the *Morning* when it happened. A shudder ran through the boat, a once familiar ripple we had all forgotten. A wave.

Rachel Davis, aged 15
King Edward VI School, Staffordshire

A WordWeam Whirlwind

by Tilly Nevin

The noise woke everybody up – the sort of noise that sends you diving under the duvet. It was the sound of a book opening; its covers clanging down; the dust rising from its well-worn pages like incense in a church spilling out of its canister. It was the sound of a person's hands turning the pages, as if the words themselves whispered as the person's hands stumbled over them. Maybe those words whispered, because they certainly shouted – meanings, metaphors; those terms you can learn that speak nothing of the thud a word can make against a heart, each resounding around the room the reader sits in, causing a mirage of daydreams; they scald the mind and eyes with letters so permanent on each reader's tongue that the mind is forever shadowed in remembrance.

Indrazade could be a word, but instead it was a name. Of the girl who lived inside the word 'possibility'. Indrazade heard the noise and did not dive under the duvet. She did not sleep, living in a word there were black lines and sometimes apostrophes. If it were a film, the camera would zoom in on the tiny figure and up the funnel of the P. Like an isometric drawing you would see the inside of the word against the blankness of the page. If you lived in a word nothing could be done except the endless reading of stories – not that that was terrible. The word 'possibility' can be found in nearly every book, as it is borne on forewords, blurbs or even in the main plot. Thus, Indrazade could jump from one book to another, consuming, ingesting novels – Frankenstein would clamber out of the pages, nodding his grotesque head in greeting; there would be the great hump of Moby Dick, shining ivory, his body dashing through waves of the deepest aquamarine – maybe Indrazade could ride. Today she knew her stories like the back of her hand. Her black figure waned to the side of her word as she peered out into the story that lay dormant in the reader's mind. Her spiky hair and pointed ears curved like a halo around her huge eyes – the whites and pupils disapparated into pitch. Her striped arms and body glittered as if studded with diamonds.

This reader was hasty; he pulled the pages so hard past they nearly tore from the glue that bound them to the spine. The wind rustled past the pages, turning them faster. It was impossible, an inhuman speed they shook at; Indrazade's word 'possibility' darted through and past other words. She saw faces agape. It was an unknown thing and it scared her; tension filled her chest and twitches cramped her legs. She wanted to run and also to curl up. She closed her eyes, but the darkness, of what she might see when she opened them frightened her more, and she could feel a scream building. But then with a rush of cool air, it was gone; that twirling, like samaras, those maple seeds some know as helicopters, departed as suddenly as it had come. Indrazade felt her terror dissolve as she began to wonder where she was. She could hear a great noise swelling up from beneath her, like a thousand people talking. She stepped out onto the page and from the corner of her eye saw other WordWeams emerging. She wandered forward a few steps – and into the story.

It was a great hall with a sign painted with *'Toad's Hall'*, filled with dancing people. She saw with a shock Scarlett O'Hara adjourning, down the central column of stairs, surrounded by gentlemen vying for a dance, wearing the off the shoulders afternoon dress, rich turquoise, slipping over the stone like a snake. The March Sisters, little women, were dancing also, with their neighbour, the notorious Laurie, and Amy's pink dress frothed as she danced with him, Beth's cheeks flushed with embarrassment like cakes with pink icing melting, Meg's piled hair curled on top of her head and Jo skipped with that long desired elegance. Edward Cullen swung his pretty, human love round as she chatted with her jealous friend, the werewolf Jacob Black. Arthur Pendragon and Merlin she saw; Aragorn, Frodo, Legolas, Gandalf offering their arms to the lovely elf princess Arwen; Peter Pan and Wendy scaled the ceiling. WordWeam Indrazade marvelled at this strange phenomenon; all the novels had been muddled. Wendy alighted to the floor and was met by a swooning Ron Weasley and Edward Cullen seemed ready to murder as Arthur tried all his courteous ways on Isabella Swan. Indrazade assumed human form quickly. She hastened around the hall – guiding a misled Arthur back to Guinevere and a bewildered Ron back to Hermione.

Suddenly a huge, warm darkness swept across the room and Indrazade saw even Puck falling asleep, looking as if death had come. Other WordWeams panicked and tried to rouse them; their power was not strong enough to wake the others. Indrazade knew what would happen if she did not wake them all. All the great classics would disappear as if they had never been there – literature would have a great hole punched through its chest. She quickly woke the two people asleep closest to her and looked into the faces of

Dorothea Brooke, heroine of Middlemarch and Tom Faggus, legend of Lorna Doone. He whistled for his ever-faithful horse, the "Enchanted Strawberry Mare". Her hooves thundered across the hall; she moved like a ghost, so fast was she it took only seconds for her to reach them; the muscles rippling under her chestnut and copper flecked skin, the blood pounding through her veins and streaming through her white feet. 'What's happened?' Dorothea asked, looking at Indrazade and then at the imposing figure of the horse.

'Who are you?' Indrazade replied, quickly, assuming her role as a bystander, 'I was just standing there and everyone fell asleep or unconscious, I don't know...'

Tom whispered to his horse, who moved her head over Indrazade, smelling her scent. He nodded. 'She thinks you're a good sort.'

Indrazade smiled softly as she saw one of her favourite stories reenacted in front of her very eyes.

Dorothea frowned.'What can we do?' she queried Indrazade.

Indrazade had a sudden idea. 'Well,' she said, 'it might work if ... just take my hand.' The two people grabbed her outstretched hands, but she could read in their eyes they had no idea what she was doing. She threw her power through them, reaching Dorothea's mind and Tom's strength – people began to wake. The awful blackness faded fast, then it rolled over Indrazade in one grand wave – and she was back, trapped, in her own word. She wished for once that she, too, could sleep.

Sometimes you may think you see something in each word, maybe if you've read too much in a day and your mind is spinning. Those words may still dance when you close your eyes – and don't ignore them. The movement of the words is, of course, the WordWeams, reliving the story that you left hours ago.

They have their own stories, but no one ever reads them.

Tilly Nevin, aged 13
Beaconsfield High School, Buckinghamshire

**‘Once upon a time in Rapland
Where words were wicked
and cool.’**

Benjamin Zephaniah

Words and Peace

By Freddie Martin

Once upon a time in Rapland
where words were wicked and cool,
two brave and fearless rappers
were locked in a terrible duel.

Drawing their swords of sentences,
striking with insults and puns,
they were true masters of their art,
their words as deadly as guns.

Similes and metaphors flew through the air
with the crowd watching it all.
Then, suddenly, a blow was dealt
and one valiant knight did fall.

Silence fell on the bloody battlefield
as everyone held their breath
he was the greatest in the land,
could this be his death?

Then finally the wounded soldier
slowly got back on his feet
and shook hands with the victor, who celebrated,
as he admitted defeat.

The moral of the story, dear friend,
is language is friend, not foe.
Imagine if the rappers had guns in their hands
how different this story would go...

Freddie Martin, aged 15
Oundle School, Northamptonshire

Rick in de Rapland

by Joshua Jackson

Once upon a time in Rapland
Where words were wicked and cool,
De rhymes dey flow from your mouth,
Like de ocean water from de fall.
And de birds dey spit wit de tune of de sky,
Singin' de raps while dey fly up high!

And in Rapland where the kids can scream and shout,
De land where de sun is gold and always out,
De slickest guy from all round town,
Slick Rick! Wit de cap on 'is crown,
Was struttin and slidin' down de street,
Spinnin', moonwalkin'! Wit de smooth feet.

His feet was on fire! Wit 'is hot shoes,
Rollin' wit Rick was like takin' a cruise,
But what did him wear? De sneakers? De flats?
No! Dem shoes him mama make for him,
Dem shoes make him one cool cat!

Dem shoes were 'im power! 'Im soul! 'Im flare!
Leave home widdout dem? Rick wouldn't dare!

If de party was live, den Rick was dere,
Wit de spring in his step and de plaits in his hair,
Him would dance for all! Den de crowd would sing
"Go! Slick Rick! Now you are the king!"

Rick was fly, dere be no doubt!
He made the girls "Ooh" and the boys come out,
Wit his tap-tap shoes and him rap-rap style,
He danced and he strut all the while.

His beat-box was safe and his swagger was nice,
But his skills wit de mic would not suffice,
At school Slick Rick weren't so sick,
Because him weren't too bright, de profs said he was thick!

Wit dem shoes at home, Rick was plain,
And until de summer month, him can't wear dem again!
So Rick would run home, cry, scream and shout,
Until one day him mama say "Rick! What's this about?
Boy, it ain't no shoes that give you the charm!
Dey ain't a part of you boy, like de leg or de arm!"

"Go to school now! And show dem you are brave!
You not a fool! You not bad! You don't misbehave!
Go now my son, and do your mama proud!
Dem books like you can't dance or sing loud!"

Him mama had a point and boy it was true,
Rick felt better now and dis he knew,
It ain't no shoes dat make YOU who you are,
Be calm, be brave den you shine like a star!

Now that's the end of de Rapland tale,
And de moral is, you can never fail!
Have some soul, have a heart! Der's nothin' you can't do...
Cause der's a lil' "Slick Rick" in all of you!

Joshua Jackson, aged 13
Belmont School, London

Look out for the Primary title

STOP PRESS

**Information for our
World Book Day 2011 – 2012
competition will be on our website
www.evansbooks.co.uk
from September 2011.**

**Register your school to
take part.**

NOTES